THE ZACK

Bozo the Clown

For Judith, and for the real Zack,
with love—D.G.

THE ZACK FILES™

Bozo the Clone

By Dan Greenburg

Illustrated by Jack E. Davis

GROSSET & DUNLAP • NEW YORK

I'd like to thank my editors,
Jane O'Connor and Judy Donnelly,
who make the process of writing and revising
so much fun, and without whom
these books would not exist.

I also want to thank
Jennifer Dussling and Laura Driscoll
for their terrific ideas.

Text copyright © 1997 by Dan Greenburg. Illustrations copyright © 1997 by Jack E. Davis.
All rights reserved. Published by Grosset & Dunlap, Inc., a member of Penguin Putnam
Books for Young Readers, New York. THE ZACK FILES is a trademark of The Putnam &
Grosset Group. GROSSET & DUNLAP is a trademark of Grosset & Dunlap, Inc. Published
simultaneously in Canada. Printed in the U.S.A.

Library of Congress Cataloging-in-Publication Data
Greenburg, Dan.
  Bozo the clone / by Dan Greenburg ; illustrated by Jack E. Davis.
    p.   cm. — (The Zack files)
  Summary: When Zack uses a magic box from Tibet to produce a duplicate of himself,
he finds that he has created more problems than he has solved.
  [1. Magic—Fiction.]   I. Davis, Jack E., ill. II. Title. III. Series: Greenburg, Dan.
Zack files.
PZ7.G8278Bo 1997
[Fic]—dc21   97-20614
                                                                           CIP
ISBN 0-448-41560-7   **2007 PRINTING**   AC

Chapter 1

I don't usually go to school wearing nose-glasses, a long trenchcoat, and my dad's Indiana Jones hat. But today was different. Nose-glasses, in case you didn't know, are fake glasses with a fake nose and mustache on them.

The reason I was wearing these things was the Three Stooges. I don't mean Moe, Larry, and Curly, either. I mean Alex, Mort, and Wesley, these three bullies who hang out near my school. They're about two years older than me and a lot bigger. I was trying to sneak past them so they wouldn't get me like they did yesterday. Yesterday they ganged up on me and pulled my pants down. And it was just my luck. I happened to be wearing a pair of old tighty-whities.

I'm used to having weird problems to deal with. Like leaving my body and not being able to get back inside it. Or meeting a volcano goddess in Hawaii and having her put a curse on me. The only weird thing about *this* problem was that it wasn't weird at all. The Three Stooges were your typical, steal-your-lunch-money and tie-your-shoelaces-together kind of bullies. You probably know the type.

Can I ask you a personal question? How do you handle bullies? My best friend, Spencer Sharp, has an I.Q. of either 160 or 1600, I forget which. He can kind of distract bullies with big words. They sort of forget what they're doing when Spencer starts talking about "retaliation" and "litigation." And Vernon Manteuffel, who's in my class but *not* my friend, cries and sweats all over them.

I'm never sure what to do. My dad says, "Zack, all bullies are cowards. If you just stand up to them they'll back down." I believe that. I also believe they might crack your head open like an egg. Now I happen to be the third fastest runner in the fifth grade at the Horace Hyde-White School for Boys in New York City. So mostly what I do when bullies start in on me is run like crazy.

This morning I was taking no chances. I had my disguise. I was wearing new running shoes. And I was taking a different route to school. About halfway there, I found one of the streets blocked off. There were these huge trailer trucks parked all over the place.

"What's going on?" I asked a policeman.

"They're shooting a movie," he said. "It's called *Drop Dead, Tough Guy*."

"I haven't heard of that one," I said.

"Well, of course you haven't heard of it. They haven't made it yet. Are you in show business?"

"Not really," I said. "Why do you ask?"

"I mean, the way you're dressed."

"Oh," I said. "This is just a disguise."

The policeman gave me a funny look. But he let me watch the scene they were shooting. It was a fight scene. The good guy was surrounded by three bad guys.

The actor playing the good guy looked real familiar, only I don't know his name. An actor playing one of the bad guys started to throw a punch at him.

"Cut!" yelled the director. The fight stopped. "Stunt double!"

The actor whose name I don't know

walked out of the scene. Another guy who was dressed just like him walked to the same spot in the scene. His stunt double.

"And...action!" yelled the director.

The fight got going again. The first bad guy punched the stunt double in the nose. Another bad guy picked up a trash can and bonked the stunt double on the head. Woof! That must have hurt.

I looked over at the actor whose name I didn't know. He was sitting on a chair, drinking a Dr. Pepper, having his hair combed.

That got me thinking. Wouldn't it be great if you could get stunt doubles in real life? Like to handle bullies at school? I turned back to the policeman.

"Excuse me, officer," I said. "Do you have any idea how much a stunt double costs?" I thought maybe I could line up somebody just for a day or two.

"Stunt doubles?" said the policeman. "Those guys make around a hundred bucks an hour!"

Rats. I only get five dollars a week allowance. So it looked like I'd have to find another answer to my bully problems.

Chapter 2

I made it to school without running into the Stooges. While I was stashing my disguise in my locker, Vernon Manteuffel came up to me.

"Nice underpants you were wearing yesterday," said Vernon. "What kind do you have on today—ones with Mickey Mouse on them?"

It was a pretty stupid joke, but Vernon didn't think so. He cracked himself up.

Vernon is this big, sweaty kid who is not my friend. Anyhow, when he gets nervous, he tends to puke. The Three Stooges picked on him for a while, too. Then one day he puked all over them. After that, they left him alone. Actually, everyone in the whole school leaves Vernon alone.

I left Vernon by the lockers, still laughing at his own joke. I went and found my friend Spencer. We headed for our homeroom.

"The Stooges got me again yesterday, Spencer," I said. "They pantsed me. I don't know what to do. What I really need is someone who looks just like me who could stand up to those bullies. Like a stunt double."

Spencer nodded. "Or a clone," he said. "That would be even better."

A clone. Hmmm. I stopped in the hallway. I looked at Spencer and nodded. *Yes.* A clone. That made sense.

Later in science class, I was still thinking

about clones. Mrs. Coleman-Levin was showing us how water expands when it freezes. If you want to know the truth, I didn't really care what happens to water when it freezes.

"Zack," said Mrs. Coleman-Levin. "Do you have any questions?" That's her way of nailing you when you aren't listening.

"Yeah," I said. "How do you go about cloning somebody?"

"We weren't speaking about cloning," she said. "We were speaking about what happens to water when it freezes."

"I know that," I said. "But how does cloning work? Maybe if I understood that, I could understand what happens to water when it freezes."

She laughed. Mrs. Coleman-Levin is pretty cool.

"Well," she said, "cloning is a way that scientists can make copies of a living thing.

All they need is a tiny sample of its body. I'm sure you've read how scientists have been able to clone sheep."

I had, but that wasn't any help. The Three Stooges picked on kids, not farm animals.

"Could you clone a person?" I asked.

"Maybe some day," she said.

"How long would it take to clone a person?" I asked. "Just give me a ballpark figure."

She smiled.

"How long would you *like* it to take?"

"Around twenty-four hours," I said.

"Well, I hate to disappoint you," she said. "But it would take quite a bit longer."

Rats! Clones took too long. And stunt doubles were too expensive. What I needed was something fast and cheap.

Chapter 3

Before I left school I slipped on my disguise for the walk home. I knew that bullies attack when you least expect it. So I was expecting it as much as possible.

It turns out bullies also attack you when you *most* expect it. I know this now because less than a block from school, Alex, Mort, and Wesley jumped out of nowhere and blocked my path.

"Get a load of Zack's outfit," said Mort.

I guess my disguise needed work.

Wesley sneered. "You look cool, Zack.

But I don't like the pants. Do you, Alex?"

"Nope, I think the pants should go," said Alex. He tried to yank my pants down around my ankles. Then Mort grabbed my nose-glasses and ripped off the nose. And Wesley snatched the Indiana Jones hat off my head. He started tossing it back and forth with Alex.

"Cut it out!" I cried. That hat is my dad's. If the Stooges messed it up, I'd be in big trouble.

"Hey, look! A cop is coming!" I shouted. The Stooges all turned around. Of course there wasn't a cop. They aren't called the Three Stooges for nothing. I snatched the hat and started running like a madman.

The bullies chased me for about six blocks. I was holding onto the hat with one hand, and holding up my pants with the

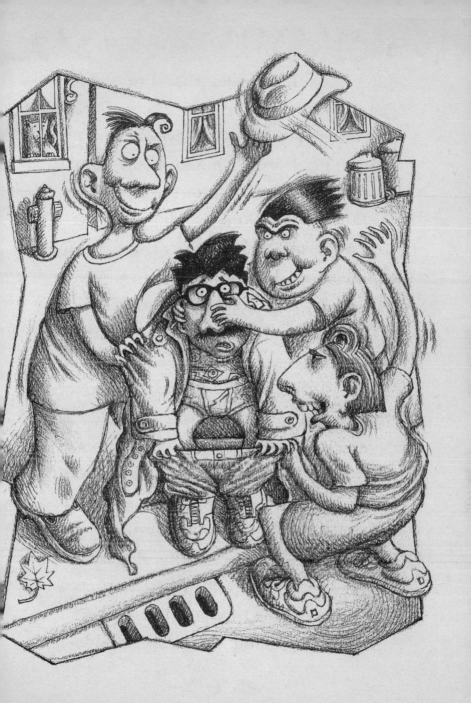

other. Did I mention that I'm the third fastest runner in the fifth grade? Well, on any other day I would have outrun Alex, Mort, and Wesley, no problem. But the pants were kind of slowing me down. I could hear the bullies catching up.

I flew around the next corner. An open gate was up ahead. I raced through it and almost ran smack into a crowd of people.

I stopped and took a quick look around. What was going on here? I tried pushing my way through the crowd. I was in a big lot filled with long tables. The tables were covered with all kinds of stuff for sale.

It was a flea market. In case you didn't know, a flea market is a place where people go to buy or sell just about anything. I don't know why they call it a flea market. I mean, I've been to lots of flea markets and I never once saw them selling fleas.

I ducked behind the nearest table and

looked back toward the entrance. Alex, Mort, and Wesley were searching for me. But there were too many people. Too many places to hide. Soon they got bored and left.

When I was sure they were gone, I crawled out from behind the table. There was a painting of Elvis Presley on black velvet for sale. And a sculpture made out of hubcaps. And a very fancy brass box. I picked up the brass box.

"You like box?" said this high, crackly voice in back of me.

I jumped about a foot in the air. I mean, I wasn't expecting anybody to talk to me.

A short old man dressed in long orange robes was grinning at me. His head was totally bald and shiny. His face had tons of wrinkles. Peeking out from under his robes were red high-top sneakers. He was wearing a button that said, "Have you hugged your yak today?"

"Is from Tibet, this box, " he said. "You like to buy him?"

"I don't think so," I said. "What's it for?"

He grinned.

"For much things. Comes with special instructions in twenty-seven languages."

"Oh, really?" I said.

He took the box and opened it. Inside was a little book. He was right. There were instructions in languages I'd never even seen before. I found the ones in English. Well, some Tibetan guy's idea of English.

"How to Do Much Things with Special Box," it said on the cover. Inside there was a table of contents.

"How to Milk Yak," was one of the headings. I didn't think I'd have too much use for that.

"How to Keep Abominable Snowman Out of Vegetable Garden," said another.

Somehow I didn't think I'd be using that one much either.

"How to Make Tulpa," said a third one.

"What the heck is a tulpa?" I asked.

"Tulpa?" said the old man. "Tulpa is copy you can make of person. Except copies are not flat, they, uh..."

"Three-dimensional?" I said.

He nodded.

"Yes. Also, not small. Same size as original. And superstrong. Nothing hurt tulpa."

I couldn't believe what I was hearing. An exact copy of me, except superstrong and unhurtable? I asked the guy how much the box cost. It was kind of expensive, but a real bargain compared to a stunt double. I'd never heard of a tulpa before. But it seemed like the perfect answer to my Stooges problem!

Chapter 4

I went home to my dad's apartment. My folks are divorced. And I spend half my time with each of them. Anyway, as soon as I got inside, I stuffed my disguise in the hall closet so my dad wouldn't see it. Then I popped my head into his study.

Dad was in there, typing away like a madman on his computer. He was working nonstop on some article for *Modern Man* magazine. It was about ways to look younger, I think. Why the heck would anybody want to look younger? Older I could understand.

"Hi, Zack. What did you do today?" Dad asked.

What did I do today? Well, I thought, let's see. I had my pants pulled down. I ran for my life from a bunch of bullies. I met a crazy old guy. And I bought a magic box. But I could see Dad was really busy, so all I said was, "Oh, you know. Stuff."

"Great," said Dad. He was trying to look interested. But his eyes kept slipping away to his computer screen. You could tell he was dying to start typing again.

I went into the kitchen and ate the peanut butter and jelly sandwich Dad had left for me. It had the crusts cut off, the way I like it. And then I headed for my room.

Probably I should have told Dad about the Three Stooges. But I wanted to stop the bullies without his help. So far nothing that bad had happened. No girls had seen me with my pants down. Only my plastic nose got broken, not my real one. And maybe tomorrow I'd have a tulpa to defend me.

I took the brass box out of my backpack and opened it. I turned the instruction book to the section marked **"How to Make a Tulpa."** I began to read:

"Greetings. So you wish to use special box to make tulpa. Very nice. But remember. Tulpa is not real person. Tulpa must not vote, operate heavy machinery, or play New Jersey Pick-6 Lotto.

"Tulpa does not need to eat, except sometimes Kit Kat bars. Tulpa does not need to bathe. Just wipe it off every few days with a damp cloth. MOST IMPORTANT WARNING: Please to never, ever, *ever* feed tulpa peanuts."

OK, all that seemed easy enough. Now on to making the tulpa.

"You now ready to make tulpa," said the book. **"Please to put photograph of person you wish to copy in box."**

I looked around for a photograph of myself. The only one I could find was my school picture from last year. It's not too great. OK, it's awful. It's kind of fuzzy and out-of-focus. My hair is all sticking up. And I have this really goofy grin on my face. Spencer says it makes me look like Bozo the Clown. But it was all I had.

I put the picture in the brass box. I continued reading.

"Now, please to shake box with great gusto."

I wasn't sure what gusto was, but I picked up the box and shook it pretty hard.

Nothing happened. I put the box down.

I figured my school picture was too stupid to work.

Suddenly, I heard something. A very tiny noise was coming from inside the brass box. Then the box started jiggling. A little like Mexican jumping beans. Then—and I swear this really freaked me out—the lid of the box raised up about half an inch, and a finger crept out of it!

I backed away from the box. I mean, let's face it. If you were all alone in your room with a brass box, and a finger crept out of it, you'd probably back away from it, too! Three more fingers crept out of the box. Then an entire hand slid out of it.

By now I was at the opposite end of my bedroom. Dad was still at his computer. But I didn't think he'd appreciate me yelling, "Dad, hurry! A hand is creeping out of this brass box I bought!" I mean, that might break his concentration.

Now the hand was followed by an arm. Then a second hand slid out of the box. The hands pushed back the lid of the box. And out climbed...*me*! I mean, it was a perfect copy of me, the way I looked in my school picture. The same sticking-up hair, the same goofy grin...

Yikes! I'd created Bozo the Clone!

Chapter 6

"Well, well, well," said Alex. "Look who's here. It's our old buddy, Zack!"

"Hey, Zack," said Mort. "Is that your face, or did your pants fall down?"

Alex and Wesley choked with laughter.

"And hello to you, big bullies," said my tulpa, grinning goofily.

It was the next morning. I was hiding behind a row of bushes, watching the Three Stooges move in on my tulpa. I held my breath. I almost put my hands over my eyes.

Chapter 5

"Oh, hello," I said.

"Hello yourself," said the tulpa. He was still smiling this really goofy smile.

"I'm Zack," I said.

I stuck out my hand to shake. Bozo took it. His hand felt kind of weird. Not like a real person's hand. It felt...rubbery. Like a monster Halloween mask.

"So," I said, wiping my hand on my pants. "Welcome to America. Where did you come from, exactly?"

"From the special box."

"I know," I said. "I just thought maybe you came from Tibet or something."

"I do not think so," said the tulpa. "But if you really want me to be from Tibet, I will. Can I have Kit Kat bar?"

I gave the tulpa a plain chocolate Hershey bar. It was all I had on me. He shoved the whole thing into his mouth and it disappeared. Wrapper and everything. I mean, he didn't even chew it!

"Okie-dokie," said the tulpa. "What do you want me to do?"

"Well," I said, "the reason I created you is to handle the Three Stooges. They're three bullies—Alex, Mort, and Wesley. They bug me every day on the way to school and on the way home."

"Okie-dokie," said the tulpa. "I will take care of them."

"Really?" I said. "These bullies are way bigger than me—I mean us."

"No problem," he said. "I have a secret weapon."

"A secret weapon? Cool! What is it?"

"I cannot tell you that," he said. "Then it would not be a secret." He giggled. Then he put an arm around my shoulder. "Do not worry, Zack. I will take care of everything."

But then something weird happened. I thought Bozo was trying to shake hands with the Stooges. But they spun around. Their eyes got very wide. And all of a sudden their feet—all six of them—lifted up off the ground.

Was Bozo making them levitate or what? Then I saw what was going on. Bozo had gotten hold of the waistbands of the bullies' underpants. He was giving them wedgies! Super Wedgies!

"Aaaargghh!" yelled the Stooges.

I guess Bozo decided as long as he had them up there, he might as well spin them around a little. Then he dropped them on the ground. They sat there for a second, dazed. Then they took off down the street.

The tulpa walked over to where I was hiding.

"So," he said. "How did I do?"

"You were totally awesome!" I said.

"Where did you learn to give wedgies like that?"

"That's my secret weapon!" Then he giggled. "So, what can I do for you next?"

"Hmmm, let's see," I said. What else could he do for me? Well, I did have a dentist appointment coming up. And I had detention next Friday. I could send him to those.

"You know what?" I said. "I'll give you a list later. But right now I have to get to school. And you should head home." I knew Dad would be out all day. Which was good. Then I started thinking. "And, uh, as long as you're home, maybe you could clean up my room? Please?"

"Okie-dokie. No problem."

"Yeah. Maybe you could hang up my clothes. Water my plants. And put my dirty socks and underpants in the laundry hamper. Think you can remember all that?"

"No problem," said the tulpa.

Boy, I thought, this guy was way better than any stunt double. He was perfect!

OK, maybe not perfect. When I got home I realized Bozo had gotten things a little screwed up. He'd put my plants in the laundry hamper and watered my shoes. And he'd hung my dirty socks and underpants on the wall.

"So," he said, "how did I do?"

He looked so proud of himself I didn't want to hurt his feelings.

"Uh, well, not too bad," I said. "I mean considering it's your first time and all."

"I can do this for you every day," he said.

"Oh, well, maybe not *every* day," I said.

"Zack, I'm home!" my dad called. "Have you started your homework yet?"

"Not yet, Dad," I called back. I signaled my tulpa to be quiet.

"Well, get cracking," Dad said.

"I will, Dad!" I called. Then I looked at Bozo. "Want to do some homework?"

"Homework?" he said. "Okie-dokie. No problem. What subject?"

"Are you any good at math?"

"Math is my best subject," he said.

I couldn't believe my luck. I got out my math homework and gave it to him.

"It's a long assignment. But it's easy," I explained. "I could do them myself, but it's a good place for you to start. If you can do these, we'll move you up to the tougher stuff."

I sat Bozo down at my desk and started playing a video game. Then I looked at my baseball cards. The tulpa was hard at work. He was frowning and gripping his pencil. When I started watching a cartoon, he looked up.

"Can I have Kit Kat bar?" he asked.

"Not till you've done your homework,"

I said. "By the way, how's it coming?"

"Almost all done," he said proudly. "Zack, please tell me. When you add four and four, is it seven or nine?"

OK. So maybe math *wasn't* his best subject. I groaned. And I turned off the cartoon. Now I'd have to stay up late and do homework.

"Boy, I sure wish I didn't have to go to school tomorrow," I said.

Little did I know how much I was going to regret saying that.

Chapter 7

I don't remember even going to sleep. But suddenly I was awake and it was morning. I looked at my alarm clock. Yikes! It was almost 8:30!

"Dad!" I called out. "How could you let me oversleep?"

Then I remembered. Dad had to deliver his article to the magazine this morning. I was supposed to get myself up. But why hadn't the alarm clock rung? I knew I had set it. I looked at the alarm button. Somebody had turned it off. But who? Bozo?

Bozo! Oh, no! Where was he? All of a sudden, it came to me how I had told Bozo I didn't want to go to school today. I started getting a sick feeling in my stomach. I pulled on my clothes and tore out of the apartment.

When I got to school, the halls were empty. Then Vernon came out of the bathroom and saw me.

"Hey, Zack," he said, "that was so gross what you did in homeroom this morning." He laughed a mean laugh.

I had to find Bozo, fast!

Right now I was supposed to be in art class. I ran and peeked in the window of the door. Sure enough, there was Bozo. I tried to signal him. But he didn't see me.

In our last class, Mrs. Dreeben had shown us how to throw a pot on the pottery wheel. Basically, she put this hunk of clay in the middle of the wheel. While the wheel whizzed around really fast, she shaped a pot out of the clay with her hands.

Today the guys in my class were taking turns throwing their own pots. So far, nobody's looked anything like Mrs. Dreeben's, which was sitting on the shelf.

Mrs. Dreeben turned to my tulpa.

"All right, Zack," she said. "It's your turn to throw a pot."

"Okie-dokie," Bozo grinned.

But instead of going to the pottery wheel, Bozo picked up Mrs. Dreeben's pot and threw it to her. I guess he thought she'd catch it. She didn't. She screamed and ducked instead. Her pot hit the wall and shattered into a million pieces. The whole class stopped. Everybody was staring at Bozo. Everybody thought he was me!

"What are you doing?" shouted Mrs. Dreeben.

"Throwing a pot?" he answered.

"Zack, you know very well I meant it was your turn on the wheel," she snapped.

"Okie-dokie," said the tulpa, smiling.

I looked on in horror as Bozo climbed onto the spinning pottery wheel. And away he went! "This is fun!" he shouted, each time he spun around.

"Way to go, Zack!" the kids cheered.

Mrs. Dreeben tried to turn the wheel off. But she just made it spin faster. Bozo was just a blur now.

"Ride 'em, cowboy!" someone yelled.

The wheel sped up and threw the tulpa to the floor. He looked a little dazed. But the goofy grin never left his face.

"Zack!" said Mrs. Dreeben. "Do you want to go and spend some time with the principal?"

"Why?" said Bozo. "Is he lonely?"

All the kids were laughing now. The tulpa looked confused. I don't think he

knew he was being funny. I felt bad for him. But I also wanted to shout out, "That isn't me! That's just my clone!"

I had to get Bozo out of school. But Mrs. Dreeben was already marching my tulpa out of the art room. They headed for the principal's office. Bozo was in there for ages.

By sixth period I still hadn't talked to my tulpa. I went and hid in the gym under the bleachers. I spent an hour worrying about what Vernon had said. What could Bozo have done in homeroom that was so gross? At this point I didn't even want to know.

When the final bell rang, I sneaked out of the building. I went around the corner to wait for Bozo.

I was so busy worrying about my tulpa, I ran smack into...the Three Stooges!

Chapter 8

"**O**h, hi, guys," I said.

I was all ready to run. But the Stooges weren't coming at me. Weird. They hadn't moved an inch. I looked at them closely. You know what I saw? Fear!

"Uh, we're just going home," said Wesley. "We don't want any trouble."

Alex was slowly backing away from me.

"Please," he cried. "No more wedgies!"

This was the moment I'd been waiting for!

"Oh, don't get your shorts in a knot," I

said. I have no idea what it means. But I've always wanted to tell somebody that. "Now get out of here."

I watched the Stooges take off. I had this really huge grin on my face. Then I turned around and saw Bozo leaving school. He had a long piece of toilet paper stuck to his sneaker.

I put my head in my hands. What was I going to do about Bozo? He was really nice, for a tulpa. And he really trashed the Stooges for me. But now he was a problem. A *big* problem. Maybe that sounds mean. But it was the truth.

I signaled my tulpa. "Psssst! Over here!"

"Oh, hi, Zack," he said. He gave me this huge grin. "I went to school for you today."

"Yes. I know." I put my arm around his shoulder. It felt weird and rubbery. "Come on, let's go home," I said.

On the way, we passed by the movie set. They were shooting another big fight scene.

"What's going on?" Bozo asked.

"They're going to shoot these actors in a fight scene," I explained.

"Shoot them!" he shouted. "Oh, no!"

I guess Bozo didn't know anything about movies. After all, he'd been in a Tibetan box all his life. I was about to explain, when the director called "Action!"

The cameras started rolling. The fight began.

Bozo grabbed my arm. "Look!" he said. "That big guy hit the little guy! More bullies!"

"He's not a bully, he's an actor," I said. But it was too late. Bozo rushed onto the set. He stuffed one bad guy in a trash can. He gave his special wedgies to two more. He was ruining the movie! The only thing that stopped him was a manhole—an open one that Bozo didn't see. He fell in, feet first!

The crew panicked. But seconds later, Bozo poked his head out of the manhole. He looked around at the crowd. "Can I have Kit Kat bar?" he asked. He was grinning his goofy grin.

I ran up and helped Bozo out of the manhole. Then a guy who looked important rushed over. "Are you OK?" he asked.

"I am one hundred percent okie-dokie," said Bozo. "No problem."

"You mean, you really aren't hurt?" said the guy who looked important. He seemed relieved. "Well," he said, "that was some stunt you pulled, young fella. If you sign a form, I may just keep it in the film."

This was all too much. Now my tulpa was going to be in *Drop Dead, Tough Guy*!

I helped Bozo sign a form. Then I

grabbed his arm and headed home. I had to break the news to Bozo. There was just no way I could keep him.

"Listen, Bozo," I said. "I hope this won't hurt your feelings. But I don't think you should, well, stay with me anymore."

"Oh, don't worry about my feelings, Zack," said Bozo. "Tulpas don't have feelings. But where should I stay?"

I cleared my throat. "Well," I said, "would you mind going back where you came from?"

"To the box?"

"Yes."

"No problem," he said. "I love the box. The box is my home."

"Great!" I said.

"Okie-dokie," said the tulpa. "Just tell me one thing."

"What?"

"How will I fit inside it?"

Chapter 9

The old guy who'd sold me the brass box was my only hope. He was still at the same booth in the flea market. Today he had on a beanie with a propeller on it.

"Hello, sir," I said. "I'm the boy who bought the brass box. Remember?"

"I see you have much success," said the old man. "That is very fine tulpa."

The tulpa smiled his goofy smile.

"Right," I said. I leaned over so I was nose-to-nose with the old man. "The thing is, sir, this tulpa is making my life a mess,"

I whispered. "I've got to get rid of him. But the instruction book doesn't say how."

"So, first you want tulpa. Then you don't. Is easy to create tulpas. Not so easy to get rid of them. Is not much market for old models. Used tulpas not like used Toyotas."

I left the guy laughing like a madman at his own joke.

Bozo and I walked sadly back home. Before unlocking the door, I turned to the tulpa. "I don't want Dad to see you, OK? I'm going to sneak you inside."

The tulpa wasn't listening to me. "I want Kit Kat bar," he said.

"Maybe later," I said. "Right now we have to sneak in without Dad seeing us."

"Okie-dokie," said Bozo.

I opened the door.

"Is it later now?" he asked. I clapped my hand over his mouth.

"Hi, Zack," called Dad from the kitchen.

"Hi, Dad," I called back. "Don't make a sound," I hissed to Bozo.

"Okie-dokie. Can I have Kit Kat bar now?"

"In a minute," I snapped. I put down my backpack. My back was only turned for a second. But when I turned back, Bozo was gone. He was heading for the kitchen. Where Dad was!

I hid behind the door, out of Dad's sight.

"Oh, hi, Zack," Dad said to my tulpa.

"Hi, Zack's dad," said Bozo. "I want Kit Kat bar."

"Sorry, buddy," said Dad. "We don't have any. But look what I have here. A peanut butter and jelly sandwich."

"Okie-dokie!" I watched as the tulpa picked up the peanut butter and jelly sandwich. *Peanut* butter? For some reason, that made me even more nervous. I tried to think why. Hey! Wait a minute! The book said never to give peanuts to a tulpa!

"No!" I shouted. I dove into the kitchen and grabbed the sandwich. But it was too late. The tulpa had taken a huge bite. Now what?

I stared at Bozo. Dad stared at me. His eyes were almost popping out of his head.

"Zack," he asked the tulpa. "Who is...?"

"Uh, Dad? Over here," I said. I gave a little wave. "*I'm* Zack."

Dad kept blinking. "Then wh-who is...?"

"I'll explain in a minute," I said. "But—"

Just then Bozo opened his mouth and let out this really loud belch. He had a weird look on his face.

"I have to split," said Bozo.

I thought this was just old-time hippie slang that meant he had to leave. Then I heard a loud, cracking sound.

Bozo split in two! There were two exact copies of me—uh, him! And they were both half the size of the original.

Dad stood there in the kitchen, staring at my two clones. He looked surprised. OK, maybe paralyzed is a better word.

"Uh, Dad," I said. "I was going to tell you about this, I really was. I was just waiting for the right moment is all."

"Hello, Zack's dad," both mini-tulpas said together. "Can we have Kit Kat bar?"

Dad tried to speak, but nothing came out.

"They're not real people, Dad," I explained. "They're tulpas. The first one came from a brass box I bought at a flea market. I created it to fight some bullies. Tulpas don't eat much, except for Kit Kat bars. And tulpas don't take showers. What you do is you just wipe them off with a damp cloth...."

I was babbling now, but I couldn't stop myself. The two little tulpas were on the kitchen chairs, trying to get the rest of the sandwich. But I was too fast for them. I grabbed it out of their rubbery little hands.

"See, Dad, what happened here is you fed it peanut butter. You're not supposed to do that. The book was very clear...."

My voice trailed off. Both tulpas belched and started staggering around.

"They don't look so good," I said.

Just then there was the same terrible cracking sound again. Both tulpas split in half. Now there were four of them! And each was a fourth the size of the original!

"We're hungry!" they cried all together. Their voices were kind of high. Like really little kids or chipmunks.

"Guys..." I said. But before I could finish my sentence, I heard another cracking sound. They split in half again! Now there were eight tiny Bozos.

"Zack..." said Dad. His voice was barely a whisper. "We can't keep them."

"I know that, Dad, believe me!" I said. "But I don't know how to get rid of them."

Dad nodded weakly.

"The tulpa was even willing to go back in the box," I said. "But he was way too big."

Just then there was another cracking sound. The tulpas split in half again.

"But...getting smaller all the time," Dad croaked.

I now had sixteen tulpas, each of them three inches high! That's when it hit me. Maybe I couldn't fit my one *big* tulpa into the Tibetan brass box. But I could sure fit all these little tulpas inside it now!

"Dad," I said, "I have an idea."

Being careful not to step on any little tulpas, I rushed to my bedroom. I got the box. I raced back to the kitchen. By that time, the tulpas had split a couple more times.

I put the box on the floor and opened the lid. Little tulpas were climbing up the legs of the kitchen table. Little tulpas were scurrying across the floor. They were making squeaking sounds. But I couldn't understand what they were saying.

"OK, guys, forward march!" I commanded. I pointed to the box.

But the army of tiny tulpas didn't listen. I tried scooping some up with my baseball cap. Dad was using a plastic cup.

"Yikes!" I cried. "One is up my pants leg!"

It tickled like crazy. I reached into my pants and pulled the little guy out by an arm. Whew!

He was squirming and squeaking like

crazy. But now I could make out what he was saying: "Kit Kat bar! Kit Kat bar!"

And then I knew what I had to do. "Dad, I'll be right back!" I shouted.

"No, don't leave me here alone!" I heard Dad yelling as I ran out of the apartment. I had no choice. I raced down to the corner newsstand and bought a Kit Kat bar. I raced back upstairs.

Dad was standing in the middle of the kitchen floor. He was surrounded by a sea of tulpas. There must have been hundreds of them by now. Tinier than ever.

I tore the wrapper off the Kit Kat bar and placed it in the bottom of the brass box.

A change came over the mini-tulpas as the smell reached their tiny nostrils. They stopped for a second. Then they stamped-ed toward the box.

My plan was working!

Dad leaned pencils against the sides of the box. The tulpas swarmed up the pencil ramps. They dove into the box and began devouring the Kit Kat bar. Soon the last little tulpa was chomping away inside the box. It was more crowded than a subway car at rush hour. I slammed down the lid.

"So long, guys!" I called. "Nice knowing you!" Suddenly, there was a soft, popping sound. A puff of smoke curled out of the sides of the box. I opened the lid. They were gone! All my tulpas were really gone! I had done it!

A few months later, Dad and I were in a video store. There was *Drop Dead, Tough Guy* on the shelf. So we rented it. It wasn't too good, if you want to know the truth. In fact, the only good scene was the fight with my tulpa in it. He sure could give one mean wedgie!

Oh, in case you're wondering, the Three Stooges haven't bothered me again. When they see me, they either sort of suck up to me or else they run away. The other kids at school are pretty impressed. They want to know my secret. No way I'm going to tell!

And I've hung onto that brass box. Who knows? Someday I might just need Bozo again.

What else happens to Zack?

Find out in

The Volcano Goddess
Will See You Now

I was busy stuffing underwear into my duffel bag when I heard somebody knocking at the door. It wasn't knocking exactly. It was more like pounding. I figured it was room service. I went to the door and opened it.

Standing in the doorway was something dreadful. A terrible looking old lady with wild red hair and crazy red eyes. She was about seven feet tall. She was also on fire, but that didn't seem to bother her. I was pretty sure she wasn't from room service.

THE ZACK FILES™

OUT-OF-THIS-WORLD FAN CLUB!

Looking for even more info on all the strange, otherworldly happenings going on in *The Zack Files*? Get the inside scoop by becoming a member of *The Zack Files* Out-Of-This-World Fan Club! Just send in the form below and we'll send you your *Zack Files* Out-Of-This-World Fan Club kit including an official fan club membership card, a really cool *Zack Files* magnet, and a newsletter featuring excerpts from Zack's upcoming paranormal adventures, supernatural news from around the world, puzzles, and more! And as a member you'll continue to receive the newsletter six times a year! The best part is—it's all free!

Yes! I want to check out *The Zack Files* Out-Of-This-World Fan Club!

name: _____ age: _____

address: _____

city/town: _____ state: ____ zip: _____

Send this form to: Penguin Putnam Books for
Young Readers
Mass Merchandise Marketing
Dept. ZACK
345 Hudson Street
New York, NY 10014